Enjoy as I have

Kate Long

THE
OWNER'S
CLOSET

THE
OWNER'S
CLOSET

Kate Lorig

Illustrated by
Don Bardole

BULL PUBLISHING COMPANY
Boulder, Colorado

Copyright © 2007 Bull Publishing Company

ISBN 13: 978-1-933503-06-6
ISBN 10: 1-933503-06-8

Bull Publishing Company
P.O. Box 1377
Boulder, CO 80306
800-676-2855
www.bullpub.com

Distributed in the U.S. by: Publishers Group West

Library of Congress Cataloging-in-Publication Data

Lorig, Kate.
  The Owners closet / by Kate Lorig ; illustrated by Don Bardole.
      p. cm.
  ISBN-13: 978-1-933503-06-6
  ISBN-10: 1-933503-06-8
1. Cancer--Patients--Fiction. I. Title.

  PS3612.O766F366 2007
  813'.6--dc22

                                    2006035396

Publisher: James Bull
Cover illustration: Don Bardole
Cover Design: Lightbourne Images
Interior Design and Composition: Brenton Beck, Fifth Street Design

First Printing

Contents

For all the people of the island where the owner's closet lives,
for my writing group,
and for Don and Jean

Preface

This book has two beginnings, and it straddles two themes. For many years I have visited the same house on the Maine coast each year. As a friend of the owner, I have always had a key to the owner's closet. This small space holds those things that he wishes either to hide or to keep out of the hands of casual visitors, such as paint, old clothing, liquor, and CDs. On many occasions my friends and I discussed writing a book about all the things that the owner's closet had seen and heard. Of course we were all busy, and so nothing ever got written. Thus the seed was planted, but it never germinated.

In 2004 I had a different adventure. This time the journey included lymphoma, with all the accompanying treatments. Thanks to good physicians, good surgeons, and modern drugs, I am currently living well with having had cancer. (It is hard to find the right verb. I do not have cancer, I cannot say for sure that I had cancer, and I hate being known as a cancer survivor.)

As part of my treatment, I attended a workshop in therapeutic writing. In my very first attempt at writing, *The Owner's Closet* opened its door. Most of the book was written in subsequent sessions, then shared with my instructor and classmates, who were dealing with their own cancers and their own closets. The only rule of our workshop was that we must treat everything as if it were fiction.

The Owner's Closet grew and took on a life of its own. Its themes of life in Coastal Maine, a simple yet complex existence; friendship; the interdependence of islanders and off-islanders; and living with cancer merge, diverge, and are braided together and separated again in ways that even I do not fully understand.

Many books start with the disclaimer, "All similarities to actual events or people, living or dead, are purely coincidental." I cannot make that claim. Although this book is fiction, it is certainly not coincidental.

Whatever you see and whatever you find, I hope that *The Owner's Closet* will bring you joy and small pleasures.

GETTING THERE

Turn left at the flying red horse.
How do I get there? I asked.
Follow the highway;
Watch the twists and turns.
How do I get there? I asked.
It is dark, and there is no moon;
Watch the twists and turns.
I am afraid. It is so cold.
It is dark, and there is no moon.
I knew that this would be an adventure.
I am afraid. It is so cold.
There is no red horse in sight.
I knew this would be an adventure.
The road goes left, and I go straight.
There is no red horse in sight.
The way is long; the night is dark.
The road goes right, and I go left.
The highway sign appears again.
The way is long; the night is dark.
A bridge appears. I see a light.
The highway sign appears again.
There is water everywhere.
A bridge appears. I see a light.
The road is straight without diversion.
Now there is water everywhere.
The flying red horse appears ahead.
The road is straight without diversion,
And I turn left.

9

I

THE SETTING

Introduction

I am the owner's closet. You might know me. I am at the very core of a vacation house on an island off the coast of Maine. My owner, a doctor who lives far away, puts all his belongings in me. At least he puts in the belongings that he does not want others to use. I keep them safe from the parade of visitors. I will tell you more about these folks later, but first I want to tell you a little about myself and how I came into being.

As I write, it is my second winter, and it is quiet. No one is here. There is snow on the porch and on the old wooden lobster trap that sits outside the window. Just down the hill is the Lobster Co-op, where the lobstermen bring their catch to be sold. I can see it clearly through the window. There is only the occasional boat, because the lobsters are mostly sleeping, and it is not yet time for mussels. Only a very few boats are in the water.

I am very, very full. There are tools, old jeans, a sweatshirt or two, hiking boots, lots of spices, an easel, a telescope, and a model of a Friendship Sloop that my owner assembled the last time he was here. But I am not here to write about what I contain—although it is my primary interest. Rather I want to share with you what I have learned. I am a silent observer. In fact, most of my visitors see me only as a door.

Only my owner and other special people have my key. They think of me as a place to store things. Now and then they unlock me to take something out, to put something in, or to just explore my contents. I am not sure that anyone knows that, besides holding things, I also listen and learn. Well, that is not quite true, because the house knows.

My house has lots of parts—a kitchen, bedrooms, and bathrooms—but I am at the center. Because all parts of the house are connected, I know everything that goes on. I speak for the house.

I was not always an owner's closet. Many years ago my space was part of a fishing cottage, what the natives here call a camp. I was built by a writer, Lewis Lewis, a man of so little fame that his books seem to have been lost to history. At least I have never seen one. Just the same, Lewis lived here for nearly 20 years. Well, he kind of lived here, because each winter, like so many others, he went south.

I remember little of those days because I was not yet an owner's closet. I was just space in a house. One year Lewis stopped coming. The house missed him. Once in a while unknown people came to stay for a day or two. One of these folks said something about Lewis having died. And so it was that the house mostly stood empty for 20 years. During this time the harsh weather took its toll. Then my present owner, Doctor Jim, saw something no one else had seen. He saw some possibilities in the humbleness of the house. He purchased the camp, and that is when my life began. Dr. Jim thought a long time about what the house should look like, and then he started to work.

Dr. Jim put in stairs. There had been none inside. He also installed floors, a shower, a kitchen, windows, and a mantle with a small boat carved into it. I have heard him tell the story of how I almost never came to exist. There was no bathroom on the main floor, and he worked ever so hard to find space for one. At last he gave up and put baths on the other two floors. In my space he built his very own closet—me. That is how I escaped being a toilet.

I was ready. I stood empty at first, and I waited to see what this new life would bring. The camp had been transformed into a house, and I had been born. Now I was ready to listen, to observe, and, most importantly, to learn. I was ready, but also excited and afraid.

The Island

During my first year, I noticed that most of my guests came for either adventure or rest. Some arrived with all kinds of fancy equipment, such as kayaks. Others came with bags of books, many of which ended up on the shelves of my house. What a few of them found, and others didn't, were the small pleasures of my island. I learned all about the island by listening to my guests and reading the *Maine Gazetteer* and material from the Island Trust that my owner left on my shelves.

First I'll tell you a bit about geography. It is 17 miles from one end of my island to the other. On one end of the island there is a bridge. They tell me it is a little like the Golden Gate Bridge, but I have never seen a golden gate, so that is not much help. On the other end, there is only water. To get off the island, you can cross the bridge, swim, or take a boat. These limitations make exploring easy—or so it seems.

Although there are only two roads up and down the island, there are lots of side roads. These lead to all kinds of places: small villages, a world-famous art school, a garden filled with fantastic sculptures made of found objects, a lighthouse, several old family compounds, and much, much more.

In many other places, my visitors say, when people want or need something, they just go down the street. There are choices of where to buy food, to purchase nails, to mail a package, or to buy medications. There are also parks, movie theaters, and churches—you know, all the things that make a place a place. My island has all of these things, but most of my guests do not want these things, or they do not find them. What they miss is the small pleasure of the search.

Most folks find food. There are two grocery stores and a small convenience store. There are numerous signs along the roads that lead a person to apples, crabmeat, mushrooms, or fresh eggs. But let's start with getting groceries. My island's food stores are a bit schizophrenic (I learned this world from a psychologist who once stayed here, and I have always wanted to use it). The stores have the day-to-day stuff—dog food, flour, bleach, hot dogs, cabbage, potatoes—but they also cater to the tastes of the off-island folks with items such as

To T-Shirt Factory

To Jordan Pond

Little Owner's Closet Island

Owner's

Town

Closet's

Tennis Court

Island

Quarry

Barred Island

Red Horse

Owner's Closet's House

Lily Pond

Town

Top Hat Islands

Ocean

15

Arborio rice, smelly cheese, and olive oil.

There is less variety in my island's restaurants. All serve the local fare, with some variations—you know, lobster, scallops, chowder, halibut, potatoes, and bread pudding (which is white stuff, as far as I can tell).

There is one thing that the island has lots and lots of—even more than most of the rest of the world does. That one thing is ways to get information off the island. There are seventeen churches for sending messages upward, and seven post offices for sending messages outward. You may wonder why there are so many. Well, when it comes to churches, I'm not really sure. From what I hear, it is a little like ice cream. They all seem to be variations on the same theme. There may be some very important differences, but they elude me.

Post offices are another thing. It seems you cannot be a real place without a post office. It is as if the federal government made the decision about what is and is not real. Actually, I guess I should not be surprised at this. If you cannot send or receive a letter, then you do not exist to the outside world. Each of my island's seven post offices has its own staff, a postmaster or postmistress, mailboxes, and announcements from the federal government.

Post offices are the center of island life. Everyone goes to the post office several times a week, and some go several times a day. At the post office news is passed from neighbor to neighbor. There one can learn who is ill, and who was seen on the pond road with whose wife. Never underestimate the power of the U.S. mail.

My guests often comment on the post offices. It seems that where they live, post offices are very big, and one spends lots of time waiting in line. Sometimes their post office people are not very kind. None of this is true here. I don't think that there has ever been a line of more than three people at any of the post offices on my island. Since everyone knows everyone else, people tend to be kind to each other and to strangers. My post offices are friendly places.

When it comes to parks, I really do not know much except that some fellow named Olmstead designed one in a place called New York. I know this because Olmstead had a house on my island, and someone left a book on my shelf explaining this little-known fact. My parks are nothing like their description of Central Park. There are no sidewalks, no manicured grass, no meadows, and no bandstands. Just the same, my island does have several parks. They are all pretty much the same. You walk through the woods on trails marked with stone cairns or painted blazes on the trees. You can get to the ocean, walk along the shore or rocks, and then walk back through the woods. Of course, there is infinite variety in nature. My guests see ferns, mushrooms, flowers, birds, trees budding, or leaves turning color. Sometimes, if they are really lucky, they see a deer. After all, my island got its name for a reason. Each park has its own personality. For example there is The Woods. As one would expect, The Woods has lots of trees and rocks. There is no sight of the ocean, just dark, mossy, mysterious woods with lots of plants and ferns. There you really have to watch for the painted blazes marking the trails because it's easy to get lost and end up at the ocean. On an island, the ocean is never far away.

The Tennis Reserve is another park, but its name has nothing to do with courts or balls. It has a lovely old family cemetery and wonderful views of the tiny islands, which look like top hats with their straight, tall pines. Another park, The Quarry, is a very special place. It is an old granite quarry where my visitors can explore and read signs explaining how men collected the stone for our national capitol. The reason that people first came to the island was to quarry granite. This activity continues today on another island just a little way from here. I can often hear the machinery and watch the barges carrying the granite to the trucks waiting to take it away.

The Pond is just down the road. Most of my guests find their way to the Pond, but I am always surprised by how many of my visitors

17

find the need to drive there. This is not true of the locals. For them the road at the side of my house is a regular walking track. The Pond is full of lily pads, and in summer, when they are in full flower, it is lovely. You can often see a great blue heron or a truly busy beaver.

Since I've learned about all the wonderful things on my island, I find it sad that most of my visitors never discover the small pleasures offered by the island's everyday world. They are too busy sleeping or looking for adventure. I do not understand why they use their time here to prepare to go back to what they left behind. It is a bit confusing.

The Village

My house is at the edge of a small town. Some call it a village, but others call it "the end of the road." It is both of these things. One of the first things that most of my visitors do is to take a walk into town. In the summer, this is usually done after dinner. Because I don't walk, I am not at all sure that what follows is accurate. It is what I have pieced together from my visitors over the years.

As one leaves the house and wanders down Pond Road, the first house on the left is wonderfully decorated. It has fairy lights, a large golf ball for a mailbox, and a statue called Mary. Go a little further, and you'll pass a church, one that advertises Mass at 10 AM once a month. Next, on a large house set back from the road, one sees the flying red horse that once belonged to an oil company. This symbol of the past is the symbol of my town.

Past the decorated house, the road goes steeply downhill to the real start of the town. Just across from the bank is a miniature village. It has tiny houses, a church, and a school, each no more than eighteen inches high. All are done in fine detail. The buildings are not like the ones in my town. They represent an idyllic New

England village. No one seems to know what the little village is doing there. It is strange to have an ideal miniature village to introduce the real village, which is truly the New England ideal. I will have to think more about this.

Just past the bank there is a grocery store that isn't open anymore. It closed several years ago and now awaits a new life.

Everyone comments on the wonderful green stove inside. I wonder what will happen to it. I know it will not fit in me.

Next comes the dock for the mail boat. Twice a day, Miss Lizzy leaves here with a few passengers, cargo, and mail. Her destination is from here, the end of the road, to Isle Haut, which is about 45 minutes away. Isle Haut is like many islands in Maine that support a small and dwindling, but fiercely independent, community. It has a one-room schoolhouse, a small store, a church, and, of course, a post office. The post office is the reason that Miss Lizzy makes the trip, and it allows the community there to survive by providing daily contact with my much bigger island.

Past the dock, the office of the newspaper, the *Island Ad-Vantage*, is on the right. I often read the *Island Ad-Vantage* when it is left on the table just outside my door. It tells of all the comings and goings and the local news of the island. Every Thursday, the entire island stops and takes ten or fifteen minutes to read the *Ad-Vantage*.

Across the street from the newspaper office is the Ladybug Shop. It, like most things here, is only open in the summer and sells things that summer visitors like to take home with them: Christmas ornaments made out of starfish, boats-in-a-bottle, and clothing with Maine themes.

The cultural center of the town, the Quarry Museum, is next. As I said before, lots of granite is still quarried on nearby islands. Inside the museum, there is a diorama showing the life of quarrymen. Unlike lobstermen, they do not have boats but instead have little trains, trucks, and automated cranes. I am told that this place is a wonder to behold. People come from as far away as Brookline to see it.

Nearby is a bookstore with carefully chosen used books and all kinds of other wonderful stuff. I understand that the owner's whim determines what is displayed for sale. Across the street is the café that acts as the town's anchor, where every single visitor to the island goes at least once. There are also places for people to stay. I don't know much about these, because my guests stay here. Further on is a store that sells completely different things each summer. The last I heard, it was selling natural arthritis remedies for dogs.

Travel on a few yards, and there is a wonderful shop where an ancient lady named Helen comes each summer to make bookmarks with pictures of the schooners that move in and out of the harbor. Besides having a bookmark for each schooner, she letters my guests' names in calligraphy right on the bookmark. Across the street is the bakery, which is only sometimes open (but mostly not). Finally, as you walk toward the end of the business district and take a turn toward the water, you'll find the town's second bookstore. It has all the latest in Maine books. You might even find my book there. In the summer, you can order the *Sunday New York Times*.

Down by The Clown, a shop where you can buy fine wine and olive oil, is the real destination for my guests on most walks. The shop next to The Clown sells ice cream. There are always many flavors: chocolate, strawberry, peaches and cream, and the all-time favorite flavors of Maine, blueberry and maple. My guests never know exactly what kind of ice cream they will find. The selections depend on the whim of the owner, the fruits of the season, the requests of summer guests, or the phases of the moon. The ice cream comes in scoops or cones, with or without sauces—hot fudge, caramel, marshmallow, blueberry, or little chocolate bits called jimmies. If time allows, the ice cream man always discusses his latest political views.

No ice cream ever gets back to me, but I don't mind, because it would not do well on my shelves. Maybe it would be all right from November to April, but by then the stand is closed, and the visitors are gone. Anyway, who ever heard of a closet that eats ice cream?

The Sea

Being an owner's closet, I do not have the opportunity to travel much. In fact, I can't travel at all. I can only observe the world through the window at the front of my house. All I can see of the outside world is the Lobster Co-op and the inlet, but these are quite enough. Every day I am able to observe the changing sea. It may be calm and blue, gray and gloomy, dark and menacing, or rolling and railing with big waves and whitecaps. Nearly every day of the year I can see things on the water. I choose the word "things" on purpose, because they have lots and lots of names, and I do not remember them all. Generally the things are boats, but, to get more specific, they come in all varieties: lobster boats, schooners, barges carrying goods, kayaks, Friendship Sloops, pleasure yachts, the mail boat, and coast guard cutters. Once in a great while, I might see a lone swimmer or a wayward whale.

I live in a fishing village, so it is not surprising to see many lobster boats. You may think that all they do is catch lobster, but they also take part in lobster races. I don't mean to confuse you; they don't race the lobsters, they race each other. The yearly boat races are a big event. In fact, they may be the largest of the island events. Everyone on the island comes out, and the lobster boats come from all the small towns along the coast. There are picnics and even fireworks. I love the lobster races. I can see only a small part of them, but I can hear the excitement. It is especially nice when a boat from our Lobster Co-op does well. This is one of those very local events that would probably not be a success in places lacking in oceans and lobsters.

The schooners are much more unusual. Schooners are large boats with several sails. One hundred fifty years ago there were lots of schooners. They brought goods to this island from someplace called

Europe. I think Europe might actually be an island somewhere east of here. Before roads were built, the schooners were like the trucks of the seas, carrying goods up and down the coast. Today the schooners have a much shorter route. They travel only a few miles up and down the coast of Maine and carry human cargo who come from around the world to ride them. The schooners stop at the islands in front of my window to give their human cargo a lobster feed or to ferry their visitors into my small town. All summer and early fall I enjoy watching their sails, which are colored black, white, red, and green. They come and go on a regular schedule. Sometimes I even hear the bagpipes played by one of the captains. It is magic! The schooners are a very big part of island life.

Yachts, however, are different. They come and go like butterflies. Yachts are sleek and beautiful, with voices that are only sometimes happy and oftentimes sharp and bitter. All in all, they are very transitory in my world. The yachts bring beautiful people from off-island to look at my island from a safe distance. They seldom leave their yachts to interact with island folks. One of my guests once talked about going to a zoo, and I think that watching yachts is a little like watching the caged animals at a zoo. I look at the folks on the yachts, and they look at me across the water, but we seldom interact.

Once in a while—actually, much more often than you might think—larger boats enter the inlet. In the last few years, I've seen the coast guard cutter most often. Someone said that the coast guard was looking for "terrorists," but this is a word I do not understand. Sometimes I also see large fishing boats. These go out for a few weeks at a time to catch swordfish and other large fish. Unlike lobster boats, these boats do not live on my island. They just enter the inlet to go to our shipyard, where they spend the winter or get repaired.

Last of all, I see many small boats—really small boats. These include small sailboats and single-person kayaks. I really enjoy watching these; it is one of my great joys. They skitter along the shore and bring laughter with them. I miss these playful friends during the winter months.

I guess you could say that boats are a very important part of my life. They provide companionship, even when there are no guests in my owner's house.

Island People

L ots of people live on my island. There are those who were born here. These folks tend to be lobstermen, families of lobstermen, or former lobstermen. Many of these families have been here for generations. There are also those who came to work in the quarry and ended up staying. There is also a group of locals who have served the island for years. They own stores, restaurants, or farms. Some are craftsmen, working as carpenters, as bakers, or as dockworkers in the shipyard. Many people do more than one of these jobs, depending on the season and the island's demands.

There is also a group of people who were not born on the island but have been living here for many years. Some have retired and live here full time. Others are artists who came here to enjoy the simple and inexpensive life while attending to their life's work. One of these artists bought an old forge, and he makes wonderful sculptures while his wife makes beautiful jewelry. They even serve as elected officials. Some of the newcomers have businesses. Many of these off-islanders started out as visitors but learned to love the island and left their other life to join us here. They will always be off-islanders even though they have become part of the everyday fabric of island life.

Many people live here only part time. They have a home or an apartment in some other place and then a second home here. They come for weeks or months each year. Some of these people, like my owner, try hard to be part of island life. They make friends, take an interest in local doings, and somehow live with a foot in both worlds. Others come and find a lovely view that they try to keep all to themselves. They build very big houses, tell the locals that they cannot trespass on the shore, and act like they own the roads, the trees, and the ocean as well as their big houses. At least they are here only a few weeks a year, during which time they are tolerated, if barely so. At other times of year, they are forgotten, and the locals trespass all they want. Except that it isn't trespassing, it is doing what they have been doing all along.

The last group of people is the visitors. These are the folks I know best because they stay in my house. These visitors, like people everywhere, are of all types. A few come and hate the island. It is too slow, too backward, and doesn't offer enough to do. These people seldom return. Most of my visitors find that they like my island and my house. Some take away a week of memories, like a postcard, and never return but always have a soft spot in their hearts for a small Maine island. More often than not, my visitors fall in love with the island and return every chance they get. Some even come in winter just to find out what it is like during the cold winter months.

Another thing that I have noticed about the island people is that they have different cultures. Those born here and those who have lived here for a long time are used to the island. They know its joys and foibles. In fact, they are so comfortable that they do not often think about what it is like to live here. The other people live elsewhere and visit here. Their "real" life is somewhere else. They find the island exotic, interesting, and restful, but they would never think of coming here forever. The people from these two cultures often meet, pass, and think they understand each other, but in fact, they don't realize that each is quite distinct. I learned all of this from my owner, who once likened island people and visitors to doctors and patients. They are interdependent, but what one finds comfortable, the other finds frightening. They learn to interact, but they may never fully understand each other. From all of this I have learned that the only reality is what each person sees and does each day.

Gaining Wisdom

By now, you may be wondering how I know all the things I know. After all, I can't go out and wander about the world. Closets don't do that. I can see, and I can read, although most of the time it is too dark to do much of that. The darkness is not a great problem because there are many other things besides books on my shelves. They tell me about themselves, and I can listen. In fact, listening is what I do best, except for holding things, that is. I listen to the stories told by all the things I hold and by the guests who come to the house. They often talk of where they have been, what they have seen, what they are feeling, and whom they know. Because I cannot travel, I find that the next best thing is having the adventures of those who have traveled brought to me.

Since I began my existence with my shelves quite empty, all of the things on my shelves have traveled to get here. They have come from across the island, the state, or the country. They tell me all about what they have seen. Let me give you an example. Dr. Jim always leaves some clothing in me. Most of this he brought from his other home, which is on the coast that is to the left of the country. They tell me it is called California. His hiking boots have taught me a lot about trails out there, as well as all the places they have trod on my island. In fact, a great deal of what I have learned about the island comes directly from Dr. Jim's boots.

There is also a pair of shorts that I find especially interesting. They are old and threadbare and have traveled with Dr. Jim all over the world. Shorts has told me stories about the south of France and about Kenya. I especially like the stories about the big gray animals with very long noses. Shorts speaks very fondly of these elephants. I would like to see one, but I do not think they live in Maine, even though Shorts was not sure about this point.

A small piece of coral lies far back in one of my corners. A guest found the coral in the bottom of her suitcase and left it here. Coral has wonderful stories. She told me that she came from a country that is very far away, a place where there are big animals that hop. I, as well as all the things stored in me, find this fact really strange, because around here our animals do not hop. They run, maybe even skip, but they do not hop, except for the rabbits. Coral tells me that she is not talking about rabbits at all, but very large animals that have powerful legs for hopping great distances. It took her a while to remember what her owner had called them, but she finally told us they were called kangaroos.

I have learned a lot from Coral and Shorts. Before they talked with me, I imagined that the whole world was pretty much the same. I quickly learned that some places were hotter and some cooler, but I never imagined that the plants and animals would be so different. I once assumed that there were deer like I see on my island everywhere. Coral was a bit like me before we talked. She knew about kangaroos but was surprised to discover that they did not live here. Shorts, who is very well traveled and knew about deer and elephants, had never heard of a kangaroo. So we learn from one another. I now know about animals that do not live here. I also know that there are probably even more animals I do not know about at all.

I also learn a lot from books. Many different ones have rested on my shelves over the years. Each book tells me about himself (books are masculine in most languages). I have learned about mysterious things, amazing things, and some really mushy things. This is because many of my guests like to read this sort of thing, and then they leave their books here. There is also a history book and a *Maine Gazetteer* that has lots of maps. The books tend to come and go. A guest will leave one, and the next guest will pick it up and take it away, but leave another book in its place. With all these books coming and going, I am always learning new things. Once there was a book of poems. I especially liked these. The poems gave me lots of things to think about. Sometimes I worry, because there is so much to know. I could be here forever and never stop reading or finding out about new things.

One of the books told me that knowing that I do not know is called wisdom. After I thought about that for a little while, I decided that the difference between knowledge and wisdom is that knowledge comes from learning things while wisdom must come from thinking about all the things I have learned.

II

FEELINGS

TRUCKS & BUSES
OVER 2 TONS USE
MAINTENANCE SPUR

Whenever I am faced with something new or unknown, my first reaction is to be a little bit afraid. After all, one never knows what terrible things might happen. Over the years I have learned that usually all of this worry is for nothing. Just the same, I continue to meet the unknown with some trepidation.

This is exactly how I was feeling during my first summer. Who would come? What would they be like? I soon found out. I had been ready only a few months. In fact my house still smelled of fresh paint. I remember that it was a starry night and quite late when I heard a car pass out front. I did not think much of it, but then the car slowed, turned around, and returned. It drove right up to my door, and two women got out. It was very late, and they seemed very happy to finally be here.

There was the tall one, Jan, and the short one, Kay. I remember listening to them chatting about their trip. It seems that Jan lives in a place called North Carolina, but Kay comes from California. She knew Dr. Jim, and he arranged for them to come. From Jan and Kay I learned how very hard it was to get here. They each flew on a very large bird to a place called Boston, where they met, and together got on a smaller bird and flew on to Bangor. Then they had to find a car and follow the driving directions given them by Dr. Jim. His directions were very simple: follow Highway 18 to the flying red horse and turn left. It seems that finding Highway 18 was not much of a problem for the women, but no one told them that Highway 18 is not a regular highway. In fact it apparently is a very irregular highway. First it turns left, and then it turns right. Sometimes it seems to double back on itself. As if this were not bad enough, most of the highway runs through dark woods with very few signs. After many miles the highway, which is really a dark and narrow road, comes to a bridge—a long, narrow, green suspension bridge that links my island to the mainland. Of course, once they got to the island, they thought that they were finally almost here, but that was not the case. They still had many miles to go, and all the while, they were looking for the flying red horse. They had been told that the flying red horse was once the symbol of an old gas station, one that no longer has gas but still retained the symbol of its past. Once they finally found the red horse, they were to turn left. After that last turn, it should have been easy to find me, because I am just up the road. But that night, it was very late and so dark that they drove right past my house and into the woods. When they realized they could go no farther, they turned around and came back. At last they found me. Apparently some things that seem simple to one person are very strange and complex for another. This was one of my first lessons.

On that first night, I remember thinking that Jan and Kay seemed very nice. They spoke quietly, made themselves each a cup of tea, and were ever so pleased to be here. They did not seem the least bit scary. At the time I did not know that we would become fast friends, and that I would become important in their lives and they would become important in mine. All I knew was that for the first time in weeks, there was a light in my window, and I was not so afraid.

Adventures

You might wonder what visitors to my house do. Everyone seems to enjoy looking out over the inlet, observing the storms, and watching for schooners. Only a few ever see the spectacular red, orange, and purple sunrise. At the end of the day, if they are very lucky, they can see the orange moon as it rises out of the sea. Of course, no one in my house can help but follow the daily comings and goings of the lobstermen. They pass by my door very early in the morning as they make their way to the Lobster Co-op and their boats. These things are all background for the daily lives of my visitors.

They come for this quiet routine of daily comings and goings, but there is much more that awaits them.

I know what to do each day. I sit stationary and hold things. What I hold may change, but what I do, day in and day out, is hold things. On the other hand, my visitors want to do many things. Each day they make a new decision about what they will do. Some people, like Jan, Kay, and my owner, Dr. Jim, come back year after year and more or less know what they want to do. I think that they call this "having a routine," although I do not really understand this word. Routine is fine because it makes life predictable. I think that this means knowing what will happen each day, but of course they don't really know.

What I really want to discuss is first-time visitors. They do not have a routine, so nothing is predictable. Maybe this is why they come to the very end of the road and turn left instead of right. For them, what to do is explore. They want to see the world of my island. Most evenings these visitors return from their day's adventures and rehash their findings. Here are some of the things about the island that I have learned from them.

The art of exploring is determined by each person: where to stop, who to talk with, and how to enjoy small pleasures. Let me tell one story I know very well. After all, Willy Wooden Gull lives on my upper shelf most of the year, and we talk a lot—but I am getting ahead of myself.

About 10 miles up Highway 18 there was once a sign—white with black hand-painted letters. "HARDY," it said. Nothing else. It stood outside a rather ordinary and slightly rundown house at the side of the road. Most people never stopped at HARDY. But a few curious or informed guests did stop there, and they had an adventure to write home about.

The Hardy house was not welcoming. To get anyone's attention one had to walk around to the side of the house. The front door did not have a bell or a knocker. The only way to raise the occupants was to bang on the door, then wait, and then bang again, repeating this action over and over. Often nothing happened. Mr. Hardy was frequently away. But sometimes, if the visitor banged and waited long enough, Mr. Hardy came to the door. "Suppose you want to see the carvings," he'd say. "Don't have much. It's late, and wood's expensive. Beech is going for ten dollars a foot." Then the visitors followed this old, slightly disheveled man to a small hut one hundred feet behind the house. He would fiddle with the bad lock and open the door wide. A single light bulb flickered on as Mr. Hardy pulled on a long cord and revealed four unpainted wooden walls, a chair, and nearly empty shelves. Here and there on the shelves were wonderful carved birds and animals. Some were only partly finished, like a bird, but without its wings completed. Others were not yet painted. The best part, though, was the finished animals and birds. These were painted in solid colors, simple and folksy. Mr. Hardy's carvings represented the essence of our island, transformed from blocks of wood. Somehow his carvings captured the feeling of tranquility that my visitors wanted to take back to their daily lives.

That's how Willy Wooden Gull came to live in my house. Many years ago some visitors stumbled upon the HARDY sign. When they arrived at the shed, there were very few carvings. Willy Wooden Gull was one of those. A great blue heron was sitting lonely on one side. A few unpainted hummingbirds that had not gotten the chance to fly south occupied the other side. Winter was coming, and wood for carving was expensive. The visitors knew immediately that they wanted that great blue heron. The man also liked Willy Wooden Gull, but his wife was not so sure. After a great deal of discussion they decided to buy both birds, although the wife was not entirely happy with their second purchase. At the end of the week when my visitors left, they took the great blue heron with them but left Willy Wooden Gull sitting on the kitchen shelf in my house. I never knew if they forgot him or just decided that he would not fit in their world. Whatever

34

D. Bardck

the reason, Willy Wooden Gull remained and soon became a part of my house. When my owner came back, he immediately fell in love with him. So now Willy Wooden Gull lives on the kitchen shelf when Dr. Jim is in residence. The rest of the time Willy lives on my shelves. That is what an owner's closet is for—to keep certain treasures away from the visitors.

But what I started out to say is that there are many adventures on my island. Sadly, Mr. Hardy is one who has passed into blessed memory. He has gone on to to carve his birds in that place where the wood is free, and the seasons are always perfect.

Acceptance

As I explained, I live in a house. This house is used by many people, all of whom pass my door. One of the things that I have observed is that everyone comes with expectations. The house in which I live is not a home to anyone. It is the other place. My house is the place to get away. My guests seem to live very busy lives. They come with the expectation that this will be a place to relax and catch up on sleep. Other guests want to escape. They come to mourn something that has happened in the past year, perhaps the breakup of a relationship, the loss of a loved one, or maybe they are just reflecting on what might have been. A few guests come in great turmoil. They hope that they can leave their problems behind. These are the guests who fight and storm. Frankly, these are my least favorite guests. I don't want their troubles, and they could not leave them with me even if they tried. Finally, I have many guests who come mainly to discover and accept the island as it is. These are the artists and writers. They try to capture a bit of our surroundings so they might transplant this to other places. Whatever their expectations, the house in which I reside is not home. Some leave fulfilled, others leave resigned, calm, healed, or sometimes distressed. All of this I have watched.

Don't they realize that the island is constant and that their expectations, and the fulfillment, disappointment, or anger, are of their own making? Even the brightest sky and warmest sun disappoint some people. They go out to enjoy the island, and when they return, all they can talk about are the "damn black flies." It's true that in the spring, black flies are pests; they bite and cause a terrible itch. All my guests have to do is come inside, go down to the water, or use Deet. But I think they would rather talk about the damn black flies and how they spoil everything, making their joy impossible.

Other visitors come expecting to walk the rocky shores, sail the inlet, or climb Blue Hill. Instead, they find that a Nor'easter bears down with a cold wet wind. The starry night gives way to heaving waves, and the moaning trees quickly lose their leaves. The lobstermen watch their boats from shore all night, hoping against hope that the boats will not break their mooring to be lost at sea or to crash upon the rocks. The boats are the lobstermen's lives.

Sometimes my visitors, who had hoped to take a walk, awake to a cold gray day. They take one look out the dormer window and decide that this is indeed a wonderful day, just the day to make pancakes before the lights go out. They light the wood stove and pull out a book. Blue Hill will wait. They might try again tomorrow, or next year, or in their next lifetime.

I have observed this phenomenon many times. I have come to think about it as acceptance of the "B" words, black flies and books. It is not me or the place that determines their experience. It is what my guests carry in their hearts and in their baggage. My role is to observe, learn, and keep the black flies out.

Rituals

I was right about my two women friends, Jan and Kay. After that first visit, they came back the next year, and the next, and kept coming. I learned that they come when the Ladybug shop has its closing sale. The Ladybug shop—so they tell me, for I have never been there—is one of those stores for summer people. It has some gifts that visitors take home and then give to a rummage sale. It carries things like high-styled camp clothing, an oxymoron if I ever heard one. It also sells stickers and candy for the kids, as well as books that people seem to like to read on vacation. Of course, it also carries lots of postcards so people can write to the friends that they are happy to have escaped.

Jan and Kay always come in the fall. I don't think that they really come for the sale. It is not that exciting. But something draws them back year after year. Because they are friends of Dr. Jim, they are special people and have my key. They always open me and hunt around for one thing or another. They sometimes leave a piece of clothing or two. I think it is not so much for storage as a declaration that they will be back. They do not use me much, but I always look forward to their coming. It gives me a chance to air out before the winter and have some last quiet company before the long months ahead.

These two have a routine. They are into cooking—especially blueberry apple crisp—and reading, walking, and buying T-shirts. By talking to someone in a restaurant, they found the most wonderful T-shirt place, although listening to them, you'd believe that getting there is quite the expedition. First they go up Highway 18, and then down Highway 1, and then take some jigs and jags. They have gotten lost more than once. If all goes well, they arrive in the tiny village of Justice in about two hours. It is so tucked away that unless my friends knew exactly where they were going and had a good atlas, they could never find it. Here in this most unlikely of places, they print the most wondrous T-shirts. I understand that many people have seen them at places like the Metropolitan Museum of Art, the Monterey Bay Aquarium, and Earth stores. I am quite sure that even though many people admire these T-shirts, very few people ever wondered where they came from. I can tell you. They come from Justice.

Sometimes T-shirt printing goes awry, and shirts are produced with wolves on the front and little brown bats on the back, or florescent constellations on the back with a dinosaur on the front. These are quite wonderful, if you're that kind of person. These mistakes are sold at great prices. My women friends enjoy buying T-shirts; they buy not just one or two, but a dozen or more. A few of the T-shirts always seem to end up inside me. It is a ritual.

I've learned that they have other rituals too. They always stop at the hardware store across from the store that prints the T-shirts. This must be a place of unending possibilities, because I have many things from there stored inside me, including crystal doorknobs, strange old tools that I do not understand, and even some old records.

But back to Jan and Kay. Unlike anyone else who comes to visit, these two are into cleaning—not just a quick swipe with a broom and sponge, but real deep cleaning. They wash the stairs, mop the floors, wash the curtains and rugs, wipe away all the fingerprints of summer, spray and wash the showers and shower curtains, and sweep up all the old dead sow bugs that seem to multiply overnight. Thank goodness they never try to clean me. I like my mess just the way it is.

I could tell them that this cleaning is for naught. Winter is coming. No one will be here and by the time spring comes, more bugs will have died and cluttered the floor. Dust will have settled; the windows will be streaked by the snow, rain, wind, and sleet. But the two women continue their ritual of cleaning. It must be some sort of a game, because they keep saying that they are earning points. For a long time I did not understand this. Then once they were here at the same time as Dr. Jim. He kept telling them that they had to earn points if they wanted to return. So I guess that this cleaning is part of the ritual. It allows them to return.

Clothing

Because no one lives in my house permanently, everyone who comes brings his or her own clothing. This supplies a never-ending point of discussion, and, for me, a great deal of humor. No one who visits knows what to wear in rural Maine. This surprises me, as it is really very simple. In summer you wear jeans or cotton

39

pants, T-shirts, and sandals or running shoes. On a very few hot days, you can wear shorts. In the fall, add a long-sleeve shirt or jacket. In winter, change to wool or fleece, and add lots of layers and boots, but even then, I'd advise you to stay mostly indoors. Spring can be tricky, warm or cold, wet or dry. You rotate the clothing from the other three seasons. Sometimes this has to be done several times a day.

There is one other spring complication: black flies. Black flies don't much like closets, but they love people. They eat you away, bite by bite. Listening to my guests, I have learned that these bites really hurt and itch. I can tell you that seeing their red Dalmatian spots and watching the yearly scratching dance gives me a good deal of amusement. Long sleeves, socks, hats, and insect repellant go a long way toward defeating the flies, or at least avoiding that itching dance.

Clothing needs here in Maine are simple, but I am always surprised by what people bring and by the discussions about clothing I hear. There was Anne with her long blond hair and blue eyeliner: "Dear, where is my pink sweater? I know I packed it. I can't possibly go into town with the tan one. It just doesn't match." I sigh; who cares? Then there was Nigel, a very distinguished gentleman with a funny accent. He was from a place call Oxford. He did not think he could go to dinner at the Fisherman's Friend without something called a cravat.

There are always some folks who arrive in May or September with nothing but skimpy shorts. Some even let their middles show. As the kids say, "Gross!" In May these folks are cold and complaining, and the black flies get them in the most interesting places. In September they are just cold and complaining.

Summer folks show up with whole suitcases full of swimming suits. They see the water and go hunting for the beach. They do not find what they are hunting for. All my beaches are rocky and not inviting for lying upon. Some hearty souls put on their suits, scramble with great pain over the rocks and into the water, only to instantly reappear as shrunken blue things. The water is cold. Only fools and children go swimming.

Other people come with suitcases and suitcases of clothing. They bring clothes for every possible occasion, including a visit by the Queen, who has never visited. They also have many changes of clothing, convinced that they will be camping, and afraid of more than eight hours of dirt. I am not the back woods. My house has a perfectly functional washing machine and dryer. My guests do not have to use a washboard, wringer, or clothesline.

I understand that many closets do not contain much except clothing. This is not true for me. As you now know, I hold many things. You may be surprised to find out that I also hold some clothing. There is always clothing from my owner, which consists of shorts, pants, shirts, and a baseball cap all spattered with paint and more than gently worn. I have heard him say that this is his favorite clothing. Go figure.

There are also other clothes. Some people, a very few, who come back year after year have my key. After being here several years, they tend to leave one or two pieces of clothing. For example, I have a pair of blue sweatpants with a small rip in the knee, a straw hat, a smock for painting left by a would-be artist, a pair of old tennis shoes, and the oddest of all, a pair of red high-heeled shoes.

This clothing is not just left here. It is lovingly left in me with the hopes and promises of its owners. You see, the people who leave clothes really, really like me. I represent another life. Just the same, they say that I represent a different life. These people seem to like my life and not only want to return, but plan to return. As a promise or a talisman of this return, they leave a piece of clothing. Thus, each year each piece of clothing is removed, worn, and then with great sadness returned.

What I want to say to these habitual clothes leavers is, "If you like my life so much, why do you embrace it only a week or two a year? My life is a good life—come join me." But they never do. I think that

41

they are afraid. Afraid that the life they dream of may be a figment of their imaginations—not a reality. This is sad. My life is very real. It is just a different life from what they usually live.

Masks

My most recent visitors, Jack and Peter, are gone, but like so many guests they forgot something. Guests leave the strangest things: jewelry, eyeglasses, shirts, underwear, and pants with holes. Jack and Peter left a mask. It is a plain black mask that covers the eyes. It is like the one worn by the Lone Ranger. This mask, hanging on my outside doorknob, reminds me of all the masks that my visitors wear.

I know that my guests do not wear real masks, usually. Just the same, they all seem to mask reality, or maybe the mask is real and their reality is a mask. Frankly it is all too complicated for me. All I know is that they arrive as apartment dwellers from New Jersey, professors from Boston, lovers from Chicago, or in one case, a minister from Nevada. As their days go on, they change their masks. Some try to go native by imitating the local folks. Some try to take over by walking down the center of the busy main street. Some make snide remarks about the quality of the local Sow's Breath wine. Others become more and more peaceful. They start out in a frenzy of trying to get everything done and then as day follows day they wind down like an old clock. Minutes turn into hours and hours turn into a day. Even their stride slows. They sleep longer, read more, make wonderful soup, and take walks in the woods, brining back bits of birch bark and balsam. They do this so that when they leave and put back on their other masks they have a bit of something to remind them of that other reality, their life on the Maine coast.

Masks remind me of something else: Halloween. This is a very big holiday on my island. For a month before, almost every house on the island is decorated—not just with pumpkins, but with witches, ghosts, grave yards, large inflated monsters, and orange and black lights. Even on the very back roads, where hardly anyone passes, the houses are decorated. Maybe the decoration is a mask, a way people have of saying that the summer people are gone, and they are once more free to not be quaint curiosities for others, but to be themselves. They do something that others also do, but they do it bigger and better, and they do it just for each other.

Maybe the decorations are masks to hold off winter for just a few more days or weeks, a way of saying that we want to have a last fling before cold and snow really take over.

Maybe the decorations are a mask of joy—a way of having and sharing fun, although everyone knows it is only temporary.

All this brings me back to the mask on my doorknob. I wonder what it was destined for—a robbery? I doubt it. A grand ball? Unlikely. Maybe it was supposed to be used for an evening of trick-or-treating. Who knows? I know only that it is a mask that has sent me musing.

The Kitchen

One of the things I have not told you about myself is that I share a whole wall with the kitchen. Most of the time this is not important because few of my guests use the kitchen. They only make coffee in the morning or sometimes make a sandwich. Few do any real cooking.

Jan and Kay, however, are really into cooking. No sooner do they arrive than they are off hunting up all the best of the local fruits, vegetables and fish. They always get apples from the apple man. One year he also had some lovely green cupcake squash, so they also got a couple of those.

That same year they went all the way up to Alan's Blueberry Farm to get ten pounds of frozen Maine blueberries, and on the way back they picked up freshly made bread from the hippy-dippy place. Their final stop was just down the hill at the Lobster Co-op. Here they went out on the dock where the dockman pulled in a big blue plastic box. It was just jammed full of lobster. He then explained how to cook a lobster and said that the rubber bands should be removed from their claws before cooking. I'm very glad that Jan and Kay had been cooking lobsters for years and did not listen, or we could have had an awful mess.

Well it seems that this time they weren't just into cooking for themselves. They had invited friends for dinner. This is highly unusual because most of my guests do not have any friends or at least not any friends from here.

Jan and Kay divided up the work. One peeled apples while the other boiled water and started mixing batter. Thankfully my owner also likes to cook, so my house has a very well equipped kitchen. In fact it has a lettuce spinner and two large strainers, along with three lobster pots and numerous other pots and pans. It even has two apple peelers. Unfortunately neither of these works.

So my guests peeled, mashed, boiled, baked, and I don't know what else. I do know that the place smelled better than it had in years. This is so much better than that damp musty smell I must endure when no one is here.

At about six the guests of my own guests arrived, and it was really nice. They sat just outside my door, and I felt totally included in the conversation. They even talked a little about my house and my island. I felt so proud. At last dinner was served: curried squash and apple soup, boiled lobster with crusty bread, and for desert wild blueberry cake with lemon glaze, followed by tea.

It was one of those perfect evenings, which are all too few. The food was good, the company was nice, and my house was warm and full of wonderful smells. These are the times that owners' closets live for.

After dinner, when the guests were gone, my door was opened and Jan put two recipes in a box on my shelf. I have thought about this a lot and have decided that one reason that people save special recipes is that they also want to save the memories of the times that the food was prepared. Another reason is that sometimes one cannot give food but one can give the secrets of its preparation. It is one way of showing friendship.

As I write this it is late winter. We have had just a touch of spring, and I am looking forward to another summer. As I wait, I thought that maybe you would like the recipes from this special dinner. Consider them as gifts from a friend. They are written exactly as Kay wrote them except here and there I added a comment.

Curried Squash and Apple Soup

1. Squash—Get enough squash to have 3-4 cups once it is cooked. Any good yellow or orange squash will do. Bake the squash in a 350-degree oven until it is soft (about 30-44 minutes). Oh, I almost forgot, before baking, cut the squash in half and take out the seeds. Put the squash cut side down in a baking dish that holds just a little water. If you want to speed up the process you can microwave the squash for a few minutes before baking it.

2. Apples (crisp tart ones are best)—Use enough for 2–4 cups once they are cooked and mashed. Peel the apples and cut them up. (If you want you can substitute 2–4 cups of unsweetened applesauce.)

3. Chicken broth or vegetable broth—Use twice as much broth as you have squash. For example, 4 cups of squash for

8 cups of broth.

4. Onion—Chop about half of a large onion into small bits and sauté (I think this means fry) in a small amount of butter until soft and clear.

5. Put the mashed squash, apples, onions, and broth into one pot with a teaspoon of curry and cook until the apples are mushy.

6. Beat the soup with an eggbeater until there are no more large chunks. If you want you can put everything in a food blender or food processor.

7. Taste and add salt and pepper to your liking.

Now it is ready to serve. You can top with chopped-up chives or a little plain yogurt.

Lemon Glazed Wild Blueberry Cake

2½ cups wild blueberries (Non-wild ones will do but are not as good.) You can use fresh, frozen, or canned but be sure they are not sweetened.

1½ cups all-purpose flour

¾ cup sugar

1 teaspoon baking powder

¾ teaspoon grated lemon peel

1 large egg or two egg whites

½ cup skim milk

2 tablespoons applesauce (unsweetened is best)

2 tablespoons melted butter (or light butter)

1 teaspoon fresh lemon juice (If you really like lemon add a little more and a little less milk.)

¼ teaspoon salt

Lemon Glaze

2 tablespoons butter or light butter

¼ cup sugar

1 tablespoon fresh lemon juice

Preheat oven to 350 degrees and lightly grease 8 × 8 × 2 inch pan. Drain blueberries if necessary. In a small bowl combine flour, sugar, baking powder, lemon peel, and salt. In another bowl mix egg, milk, applesauce, melted butter, and lemon juice until well blended. Add egg mixture to flour mixture, folding gently. Do not overmix. Batter will be stiff-gently blend in blueberries and spread batter in pan. Bake 30-35 minutes. If berries are frozen, add 5-10 minutes to baking time.

When cake is done, pour lemon glaze evenly over top and return cake to the oven and broil for 3-5 inches from the heat until glaze begins to bubble. Be careful not to burn.

Lemon Glaze

Melt butter, stir in sugar and lemon juice. Cook and stir over low heat until mixture is bubbly. Remove from heat and follow the above directions.

Serves 9 (also great for breakfast)

From the 2004 Wild Blueberry Association of North America. www.wildblueberries.com

Ordinary and Exotic

High up and way back in a corner of one of my shelves is a spiny seashell. I have no idea how it got here. Someone must have brought it from someplace else, for it does not belong here. Here, the shores are rocky, and the waves and tides are fierce. Few shells remain intact, and none of them have spines. Our shells are ordinary. They are smooth, broken, and usually very dull. They are not at all like the exotic creature in my corner.

Some of my visitors are like this kind of shell. They are beautiful, well turned out, and exotic. They try hard to adapt, even trying to sound like the island folks. This is something no one who was not born and bred in downeast Maine will ever accomplish. They sound so silly trying.

Others come and try to bring their other lives with them. Of course they all bring their other lives with them—some more than others.

I remember Sam and Susan. They decided to make apple crisp. I rather liked them. They were doing something ordinary. Something I understood. All the ingredients were here—apples, flour, butter, and sugar. They were up to their elbows in apples and flour when they discovered that they had no cinnamon.

They put on their sweaters and set out in search of cinnamon. The yellow house next to me was empty—summer folks live there and they had left weeks ago. No one was at home at the house across the street, the one with the three-foot golf ball for a mailbox. At the third house, an old lady answered the door. When my visitors explained that they were out hunting for cinnamon, she invited them in. What a surprise. This house, which looks very ordinary from the road, has windows spread across its back allowing a view of the entire inlet. Spectacular! There is a lesson to be learned. Don't make judgments on what you first see.

Once inside, Sam and Susan were invited to sit down and enjoy the view. The woman seemed happy to have visitors this late in the season. Seems she was born on the island. Her name was that of an old and important island family. Her husband had recently died. She loved her house and did not want to lose her independence. She shared her fear that she might have to go to the island nursing home. She chattered, and they listened. Over the course of an hour or so, Susan and Sam shed a bit of their own trials and worries, and they became just a little bit a part of this place. Two cups of tea, some cookies, and several hours later, they left carrying their precious cinnamon and promising to return with apple crisp.

No, this is not an exotic place. We have no shells with sharp spines. This is an ordinary place. This is a place of smooth shells, apple crisp, and neighbors who hand out cinnamon even to those from far away. Off-islanders can never really become island folk. But if they ever need cinnamon, there is just a chance that they will find the spice they did not know they were looking for.

III

EXPECTATIONS

Road Blocks

Some of my visitors can never find any joy. For them life is just one roadblock after another. One young couple, the Grays, Greg and Lucille, went off one morning to explore the peninsula. For most of my visitors this is a happy trip but I was a bit worried about the Grays. This was their first visit, and from the moment they walked in the door nothing was right. The stairs were too narrow, the shower too small, and they could not find any coffee.

I waited all day to hear what they had done and then began to worry. The sun had set more than an hour before I heard footsteps on the stairs and the key in the lock. It seems that they had stopped at the Fishermen's Friend to buy some chowder. I heard them discussing their day over dinner. This is my favorite part.

The going was much slower than they had expected. They kept coming upon **Flagman Ahead** signs. I had heard a lot about these from other visitors. They seem to annoy everyone. At this time of year, before the rush of summer people and after the winter snows, all the roads are repaired. Repairing roads requires big trucks and other huge machines to scrape the road, bring gravel, pour tar, roll the tar, and, finally, paint the lines. It is impossible to repair a road and have traffic on it at the same time. This is where the flagmen come in. It is their job to stop the few cars that venture out. When you see the

Flagman Ahead sign, you stop. You wait and you fidget. (Unless you look up and see the budding trees and clear sky.) Then you go.

When the Grays set out they did not know where they were going but were annoyed just the same that they were being stopped and kept from getting there. The first time they were stopped they were trying to cross the bridge. "Why do they have to fix all the roads now?" they asked. After waiting a few minutes they continued on, only to be stopped again by **Flagman Ahead**. Another stop, this time for a large paving machine followed by a steamroller. My guests did not know where they were going, but they certainly were not getting there by being stopped. They finally went down another road, but this was not where they wanted to be either. They said that the whole day was a disaster. At last they decided to turn around and stop for a drink in Blue Hill. **Flagman Ahead**. This one was just a short stop to let a dump truck through. "Why now? Why us?" The whole day was wasted even though they did not know where they were going.

As Greg and Lucille discussed their day, I listened and was sad because I knew what they had missed. They had never seen the yellow rowboat on the inlet. It sits there like a prize photo waiting to be taken. They did not know where they were going, and they did not know that they could already be there. All they saw were flagmen.

A Walk in the Park

Recently I had some first-time visitors named Nina and Roger who, like all first-time visitors, felt that they had to see everything there is to see in one week. In advance, they carefully planned each day. One day they would go to Castine. This is a picture-book village about an hour from here. It is full of authors, a school for young people who want to go to sea, and lots of folks who like to live the good life. On another day Nina and Roger wanted to see Isle Haut, and on another they planned to go to Belfast. But they end up not seeing the small treasures: the woods, the quarry, and the wonderful old forge.

One day Nina and Roger went to Acadia National Park. They were using a map that showed it to be only fifteen miles away. This is actually true, but those fifteen miles are all water, and there is no bridge or regular boat service. Thus, to get to Acadia means driving seventeen miles to the end of the island, another twenty miles to Blue Hill, then twenty miles to Highway 1, on which they must drive thirty miles north and finally ten miles south. You can see that Acadia is near as the crow flies, but very far if you're driving there. Seems that my visitors had many adventures. First they found the L.L. Bean outlet store. Actually it is hard to miss. It is located right on Highway 1, which is almost the only way to reach Acadia. After a stop for what they called "shopping therapy," which resulted in a new pair of hiking shoes and red flannel pajamas, they continued to the park.

Somewhere, maybe in the *New York Times*, they had read about having tea and popovers at Jordan Pond. This was their destination. Why they wanted to go to a beautiful park just to go inside and have tea is beyond me. You never know with people.

When they arrived at the tea place, they discovered that everyone else who was visiting Maine had also read the *New York Times*. The wait time for tea was an hour and a half. It must be very good tea and popovers because they decided to wait. Since they were waiting in a national park, they asked a park ranger what to do. He suggested that they walk around Jordan Pond.

Before continuing with the story, I must tell you a little about Maine ponds. They are not small backyard ponds or even duck ponds like the kind found in city parks. I know about city ponds because some child left a book on my shelves called *Make Way for Ducklings*. Jordan Pond has a circumference of about three miles. At least that is what the *Maine Gazetteer* on my shelf says. Maine ponds can be quite large. In other places they might be called lakes. I guess this is a matter of perspective.

Nina and Roger set off on the three-mile walk. No problem; they were quite fit. But apparently, several of the other tea and popover customers decided to walk around the pond while they waited as well. Many of these folks did not look at the *Gazetteer* and, more strangely, they did not look at the pond. They did not know that walking around Jordan pond means walking around a three-mile body of water. In addition, they did not realize that they were no longer in Kansas, where things are flat and there is often concrete. The Maine terrain is dirt with lots and lots of roots, and at the edge of the pond, it is often wet. In some places there are wooden walkways to get over the wet and mud, but in other places it is just the natural wet and mud.

Many of the people who wanted tea and popovers were triangular and somewhat rotund. They came dressed for tea at the Ritz, not a walk in a Maine national park. Some were wearing sandals, and others were wearing high heels. One of the men even had on a jacket and tie, and several of the ladies were wearing flowing skirts. Dressed like this, you would think that after ten minutes or so, these folks would see the problem and retreat back to the garden or park benches.

However, it seems many of them had a distorted view of their own reality. (I have learned that this is a common human problem.) Nina and Roger found themselves stuck behind a party of portly men and women wearing the most inappropriate clothing: white shirts and ties for the men, and dresses and open-toed high-heeled shoes for the women. The walkers struggled with the roots, and soon they were thirsty, but they had not brought water. Perhaps they were expecting drinking fountains. They began to complain about the roots not being removed or the water not drained and then wondered aloud why there was not a nice smooth grass path to follow. They seemed to think that Maine should be just like home. Nina found this irritating and commented under her breath, "They should have stayed at home."

Those portly people never saw the wildflowers, heard the birds, or enjoyed the white birch standing against the dark ferns and pines. They never saw the twenty varieties of mushroom. They never smelled the balsam. They also refused to get out of the way to let my Nina and Roger or anyone else pass. After about a half hour the portly ones finally took a rest among some shiny green leaves at the side of the trail and complained loudly about the lack of benches. At last Nina and Roger were able to continue at their own pace and enjoy the reflections of the sun off the pond.

Later, at the tea place, my visitors got their popovers, which were well worth waiting for and all the better for the walk. The portly ones finally returned from their walk. They were hot and sweaty. One lady had broken the heel of her shoe. They continued to complain loudly, saying that they would never return. Because they were so slow on the walk around the pond, they missed their teatime and had to wait again.

I head all of this when Nina and Roger returned in the evening. They had a good day but said that the next time, they would go somewhere that was a little less populated. One thing I have noticed is that first-time visitors often go to Jordan Pond, but return visitors seldom go.

Cross-Culture Communications

One of the things I have noticed is that many of the visitors to my house come looking for excitement. This always confuses me because I am not exactly sure why anyone would come to this distant island looking for excitement. For this one should go to Bangor.

The people who do best here, the ones who come back year after year, are those who come seeking only small joys and small excite-

ment. Just last week Jan and Kay showed up again. They were a little late in coming this year. The Ladybug sale was two weeks ago. I heard them say that Dr. Jim was coming in a few days. Maybe he will empty me out a bit.

My friends went straight to bed when they arrived. Because they never arrive until late, this has become a ritual. Jan went upstairs to the tiny bedroom with the dormer window, and Kay went downstairs to the cave. The cave is my house's bottom floor, which is built into the side of a hill so it is actually part basement. It has a row of windows looking over the lobster fishermen's Co-op. The washer and dryer also live in the cave. It is a cozy arrangement, or so they tell me, but very few guests choose to sleep in the cave. Kay seems to really like it. She always comes and makes it hers.

When Kay and Jan are here they meet just outside my door for breakfast and discuss what they want to do that day. Because this was their first day, they decided to walk down to the village. They wondered if the bakery was still open. It wasn't. The walk to town took half the day. They went shopping. Seems that they do a lot of this. They came back with a few books and a funny calculator that looked like a box of crayons.

They still had not bought any food, so they decided to drive up the island, stop at the store, and get some apple cider from the cider man. If they had enough time they planned to drive up the peninsula to Alan's. This is the blueberry factory where one can buy big boxes of wild blueberries, either frozen or canned. They set off but were back in just a minute or two. I heard them on the phone.

Their rental car had a flat tire, so Jan called the rental car emergency service. They should have just asked a neighbor to help, but I couldn't tell them that. Someone in Utah answered the call. I am not exactly sure where Utah is. Jan explained the problem. What followed was a very strange conversation. It seems that Utah is very different than Maine.

The guy at the call center asked, "Exactly where is the car?"

Jan replied, "Deer Isle."

Utah: "Where is that?"

Jan: "Maine"

"Maine . . . . I understand but exactly what is your address? I need it for the garage."

Jan answered, "There is no address. Everyone will know. Just take the second right after the flying red horse at the end of Highway 18."

Utah: "What is the cross street?"

Jan: "It doesn't have a name."

56

Utah: "It has to have a name."

At this Kay got into the act and coached, "Tell him that we are at the corner of Pond Road and Lobster Co-op Drive."

Utah: "Sorry, but I can't send a truck without an exact address."

Kay, coaching: "Tell him it is the anchor house."

Utah: "Anchor house is not an address."

Jan made up an address. "OK, OK. We are at 122 Pond Road."

Utah: "Why didn't you say so in the beginning? I'll send a repair truck. Wait by the phone."

Twenty minutes later the phone rang.

"Hi I'm Tony with Triple A in Bucksport. Are you the ladies with the flat tire?"

"Yes!"

Tony: "Where the hell is 122 Pond Road? I have never heard of it. Ain't no addresses down there."

"Just turn left at the flying red horse, and then we are the second right."

"You all in the anchor house? Why didn't you say so in the first place? I'll be down in about an hour."

While they waited for Tony, my friends discussed the difficulties of cross-cultural communications. Seems like the folks in Utah are a bit different then the folks here. They speak the same language and everything, sort of, but they sometimes just don't understand.

And so their day began again after lunch. They finally took off with a patched tire in search of apple cider. In fact, this is part of their yearly ritual. My island has the best cider in the world, but only for a very few weeks each fall. The cider is made in a washing machine from Macintosh and Cortland apples grown from hundred-year-old apple trees that have survived many a Maine winter.

Every year my friends have to search again for the cider. Like everything else around here, nothing is obvious. You go up Highway 18 until you see the handmade sign that says "apples" and hangs on a tree off the road. Look quickly or you will miss it. If you get to the Island Nursing Home, you have gone too far.

Once you spot the sign, turn off onto a narrow pot-holed road and go down to the end. Actually, it does not end; it just narrows, turns to dirt, and skirts the orchard before becoming a driveway at a large barn with a wringer washer outside.

If cider is available (and sometimes it's not), the barn door will be open, and you can go in to find boxes of apples and a sign stating that the cider is in the old refrigerator. The sign says "Please do not take more than two gallons. Leave your money in the cardboard honesty box." This box once held size-eight shoes.

The day of the flat tire, my friends were in luck. The barn door was open, and there were several jugs of cider. They quickly uncapped a half-gallon jug and drank directly from the container right then and there. Now their vacation had really begun. They knew they were in Maine. They felt sad that the guy in Utah did not understand about an anchor house, cider made in washing machines, and the pure joy of that first taste of cider in an old barn. As I think about this I have a new thought. I wonder if there are small joys in Utah that I do not understand.

Decisions

As I think back, I remember one particular storm. It was not a gentle little storm but a really big whopper. Even the fishermen stayed inside. The sea was boiling, and then, as fast as it had come, the storm continued on north to Halifax. The next day the sun was out, and all was calm.

A couple from Florida—an older man and his wife—had been visiting all week. As I listened to them I learned they had never been to

Maine before. They came up to get away from the summer heat. I found this rather amusing because many people from my island go to Florida to get away from the cold. I guess that some people are never happy.

The day after the storm my two visitors awakened a little late and made French toast for breakfast. All week long they had been talking about walking to Barred Island. They decided that this day was the day. I am not sure how they knew about Barred Island; I suspect that they talked to one of the locals. I do know that they understood that they had to check the tide tables before starting the walk. Barred Island is separated from my big island by a sand bar, and one can walk to it only when the tide is low and must return before the tide rises. If walkers miss this key point they do not get there at all or have to stay and spend eight hours on the small exposed rocky island.

After consulting the local weekly, the *Island Ad-Vantage*, which publishes the tide tables, my visitors found that they were in luck. Low tide was at 11:33 AM. So they set off on their adventure. When they returned in the evening, this is what I heard.

The first part of the journey is through thick woods. That day they were fresh and wet, and smelled strongly of moss, spruce, and that most wondrous of all smells, balsam. The leaves were turning color and those that were still left after the storm were gold and red. Many leaves of the same colors were scattered on the ground. Sadly some leaves were already brown and dead. My visitors noted that mosses of many types were on the ground and rocks and the ferns were thirsting for water after the dry summer. They also saw lichens and other plants they could not name. The path was rocky and strewn with the roots of the many trees, which were forever trying to take over the path. Looking up, down, and around, they explored the roots and stones, gazed at the birds that were hurrying to fly to warmer places, and all the while watched for the blazes on the trees and the rock cairns that marked the way.

The trees parted and the sand bar appeared. At the beginning of the bar they found the first treasure washed up by the storm: a whole undamaged lobster buoy with green and yellow bands lay on the sand. Each lobsterman has his own set of buoys and pattern of colors to tell his traps from all the other traps. They quickly crossed the sand bar to Barred Island. The island is the home of albatross, seals, and bald eagles. That day, its shores were full of a wonderful repository of gifts. Old and not-so-old lobster traps, buoys in many colors, some whole and some half, a fishing net, and a small broken three-legged wooden stool all stood waiting to be gathered. The couple also found a bottle, without a note inside, but with a sand-blasted texture that only weeks at sea can give to glass. They decided that it was just the thing to pick up and take home. The bottle got no further than my house. The next day the couple left and did not take it with them. They said that it belonged here. The most important treasure for them was the memories they had gathered.

Expectations

Peter and Jack had been talking for days about visiting Shore Home. It seems they were not really interested in my island or me. What they came for was the Shore Home. At first I did not understand. The house in which I live is on the shore. It is a very fine house and certainly a long way from the place called Fargo that these guests called home. But all they talked about was the Shore Home. It seems that they had been trying to get there for years and could not get in. I did not understand. It is pretty easy to get into most houses if you have the key. Of course you can break in, but my guests did not look the type to do that.

One day Peter and Jack packed up half their stuff and were gone. I sat empty wondering what was happening. I supposed that they had gone to the Shore Home. Then I realized that they left a newspaper clipping on the table in front of my door. It was from something called the "Travel Section."

Reading this clipping, I learned that the Shore Home was a very fancy inn located on an island about 45 minutes from me. Lots of my guests go to the island, but not the Shore Home. The article described this home in great detail. It is a very old home built by some of the island's early residents. Over the years many people have lived there, including a very rich man from New York. For a short while it was a house of ill repute. In time it had become a bit rundown. A young couple from far away bought it and restored it. The two were supposed to be very good cooks. The article talked a lot about the food, all fresh and wholesome.

I became a bit confused. This Home place sounded nice, but it didn't sound much different than me, even though it was on another island, and one had to take a mail boat to get there. As I mentioned earlier, the mail boats around here take mail, passengers, and goods from the end of the road to outlying islands. Depending on the need and time of year, they go once or twice a day, or sometimes a week. The only difference I could see between this fancy-shmantzy Shore Home and me is that here the guests have to make their own bed and cook. Of course they can go to any of the restaurants in town.

I sat empty for a couple of days thinking about my guests. It was not nice weather. It rained and the wind blew. Finally they came back and seemed surprisingly happy to see me.

It seems that their long-awaited adventure had become a misadventure. As I listened, this is what I learned. The Shore Home was very nice at first, but because of the cold and rain, everyone came indoors early. Because the Home was keeping to its rustic past, there was no electricity. I find this very strange, because they did seem to have toilets that flushed. Why one would keep to the past without having outhouses is beyond me. I'm glad that my house has both toilets that flush and electricity.

The Shore Home is lit by kerosene lamps. This creates something called "atmosphere." My guests thought this was just fine and even "charming," except that the wicks were not put high enough to provide enough light for reading. Even Abraham Lincoln read by the light of a kerosene lamp. Putting up the wick is not hard, but rather than make my guests comfortable, the owners of the Shore Home preferred to maintain the "atmosphere" and not have enough light.

I came to this conclusion when Peter and Jack talked about other parts of their misadventure. Apparently all the chairs and couches had sprung bottoms. My guests spent a cold, dark, wet day without enough light to read and sitting on uncomfortable sprung bottoms. They did say the food was good, however.

At a certain point, all the guests at Shore Home went to bed, and the owners retired to their own home, which was some distance away. I think that they wanted to read, because they had light. My guests went to their lovely room and climbed into a huge bed, only to find that there were no blankets. You get the picture: dark, quiet house, cold rainy night, only a small light to find the flush toilet down the stairs, and no blankets. What was worse was that there were no owners to find them blankets. So my guests put on all their clothing and spent a miserable night. The next day the Shore Home's owners seemed to take this all as part of a big joke. They did not remember that even in the olden days, people had blankets.

From the Shore Home Peter and Jack made their way back to my house. I made them very happy. The bottoms of the couches in my house are not sprung. There is heat, light, blankets, and, just down the hill, lobster to eat.

One thing that I have noticed about expectations is that reality is often very different from what people imagine.

IV

ANOTHER YEAR

Garbage

As I think back over the many years of visitors, there are many stories, some of joy and many of trauma. One thing remains constant—the garbage. I understand that in many places the garbage is gathered together and placed on curbs, and, as if by magic, it disappears. I have no idea what happens to it. It is just gone. But this is not true of our garbage.

The jetsam and flotsam of the lives that pass through my house, coffee grounds, toilet paper rolls, plastic bags, newspapers, orange peels, broken chairs and screens and lamps—the list goes on forever—these things collect and collect. Sometimes they are placed in cans and immediately toppled over for inspection by the local squad of raccoons. The one thing that does not happen to our garbage, however, is a disappearing act.

For garbage to move, it must be placed in a car and taken to the dump. Actually, I think that they call it a transfer station. Although I am not sure what is stationed there or to where it is transferred.

I have heard tell that the trip to the dump is high adventure. Finding the dump is the first phase. There are two dumps, but only one will take our garbage, and then only if you know the password to tell the dump guard. He is a nice man, our dump guard. He recycles lots of our junk and makes money to give scholarships to island kids.

Once past this all-important public servant you arrive. There are piles of garbage everywhere. If you happen to have anything that might find a home somewhere else, it goes into the big tin building. Maybe this is what is meant by transfer station. Cans and bottles have their own pile, old tires to the right, bed frames and broken furniture to the left, and newspapers up the hill. Anything else goes into a big stationary machine.

And so the garbage is moved, just like the Lone Ranger said to Tonto while the William Tell overture played in the background, "to the dump to the dump to the dump, dump, dump."

Now, if you could talk to an owner's closet, you might ask (but probably would not), "Why are you telling me about the dump?"

The answer is simple. I have observed that most of the people who come to my house have garbage that belongs in the dump. I do not mean old clothes and broken suitcases. What I mean is that many of them are carrying around old junk: hurts, anxiety, pain, or wishes for what might have been. This junk clutters up everything, and there is no space for quiet peace or joy. They come here, in some vague way hoping to get rid of this junk, but most of them do not.

What is the problem? They do not know where to dump their stuff. They certainly do not know that they have a choice of ways to dispose of the junk. If they do discover a way to get rid of what they do not want, a gruff dump man often stops them. A very few take the effort to sort their junk. They send most of it to the transfer station, and often leave with something wonderful to replace what they have left behind. From listening to my guests, I know that these trips are never easy, but they do seem to have benefit.

I have also observed that not all junk can be left behind. There will always be some clutter, but this can often be organized so as not to get in the way. Those who make the effort to sort the junk and choose to leave some behind seem to have a lighter load.

Maybe

By mid-September, all my summer guests are gone. It is a quiet time when I look forward to the October arrival of Jan and Kay. Early fall is the time when the lobster season starts to slow down. Maybe I should tell you something about lobsters, about the interaction between the guests and the lobsters.

"Maybe we should cook lobster tonight." Almost all of my visitors

say this at one time or another. After all, one reason that my visitors come to Maine is to eat lobster—except of course those vegetarian types. Now, not all lobster eaters are lobster cookers. The lobster eaters who are not cookers go elsewhere to find their lobster. I do not know much about this. What I do know about is lobster cookers. I have observed a lot of them. In fact in this house lobster cooking is a ritual. I will try to describe it the best I can.

Step One: Getting the Lobster

The first part of the ritual involves getting the lobster. There are two ways of doing this. You can catch your own or go to the Co-op. Catching your own lobster takes a bit of work. First you must have a lobster boat, lobster traps, smelly lobster bait, and rope, and of course, lobster buoys. Without the buoys you cannot find your lobster, even if you do catch it. You also need to know where the lobster lives, how to drive the boat, and how to bait the trap. You get the idea.

The shorthand of catching your own can be described as follows: First you set out lobster traps—large cage-like boxes covered with net with an opening in one end and a smaller opening in the other end. Bait, usually smelly dead fish, is placed in the trap, and then the trap is lowered on a very long rope into the water to the bottom of the sea. (I think that this is where lobsters live.) A buoy is tied to the top end of the rope. The buoy is color-coded, kind of like brands on cattle, so that each lobsterman can tell which trap is his or sometimes hers. It is also very important to remember the general area where the traps are laid.

Mrs. or Mr. Lobster enters the trap, and, because the front door is a net funnel, he or she cannot leave. If the lobster is under legal size, and if it is smart enough, it can leave by the back door.

The next day you go back to the same place where you laid your traps to hunt for your lobster trap among the thousands of other lobster traps. This is where having your own private color-coded buoy really pays off. You pull up your trap and voilà, with lots of luck you have a lobster. Now you have to keep it alive and happy until you are ready to cook it.

Very few of my guests catch their own lobster. Instead they go to the Lobster Co-op. This is much easier. If you go out the front door of my house and just walk about 300 steps downhill to the Co-op office, you meet Jenny, the lady in the office who does just about everything but catch lobsters. She is there almost every day when it is not storming and when there are boats in the water.

The Co-op is there to serve the lobstermen. They bring their catch to the Co-op, where it is stored in underwater pens. Trucks come from Bangor, Portland, and even as far away as Boston to take the lobsters off the Island. Some go to stores, some to restaurants, and some get to fly to such faraway places as San Francisco and London.

When my guests enter the Co-op they ask Jenny for lobster. She asks how many and what size, and tells you if they are soft shell or hard shell, depending on the time of year. She helps my guests to clarify what they really want. She then gives them one or more bags and sends them to the dock.

The guest walks a few more steps onto the wooden dock that leads to the lobster pens. Here they find the dockman. Thanks to Jenny, my guests are now experts, and they ask with assurance for two pound-and-a-halfers, hard shell, please. The dockman nods sagely. He is never fooled by the pretend expertise of off-islanders. He opens the hatch of the holding pen and with a long pole he pulls out the lobsters and puts them in the bag. The lobsters' pincher claws are held together with rubber bands so they will not damage my guests. As they leave the dock, the dockman often advises my guest to take off the rubber band before cooking the lobster. Step one of cooking a lobster is now complete. The lobster has been gotten.

Step Two: Cooking the Lobster

I know more about cooking lobsters than getting them. I have observed the cooking many times. My guests rummage around the kitchen and finally find the large back-and-white enameled lobster pot. If there are many guests and many lobsters, there is a second pot under the stairs, but few guests find it. The pot is filled with water and set on the stove to boil. They wait for the water to boil. This can take a long time, a very long time, because this is a very big pot. I have observed that putting the lid on the pot speeds the boiling.

Then comes the hard part. The live lobsters, with rubber bands still on their claws, must be dropped into the boiling water to cook. Some of my guests suddenly decide to take the lobsters down to the shore to let them go. Of course, lobsters don't live on the shore and don't go, but my guests seem to feel better.

Once the lobster is in the boiling water it relaxes a little, like being

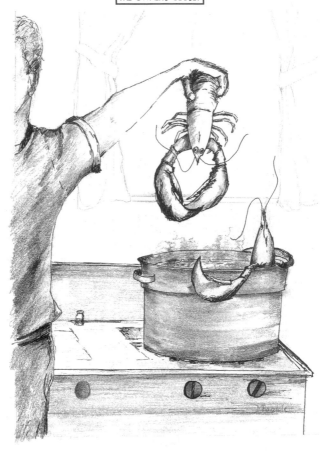

in a hot tub, and quickly turns red. Thankfully lobsters do not scream or thrash around, although some of my guests are not quite so well behaved. All in all it seems like a good way to go.

Now the guests must wait again. The water has to boil again and again this takes more time then anyone expects. Finally it boils and then the lobster must cook for exactly seven minutes. My owner, Dr. Jim, swears by seven and so I repeat it here. I do know that not one of my guests has ever complained of rare lobster.

At this point the lobster is removed from the pot. You would think that the hard part was over but this is not the case. Lobsters are one of the few foods that are easier to cook than eat.

Step Three: Eating the Lobster

You have probably never wondered what an owner's closet does for fun, but I am going to tell you anyway. We watch off-islanders eat lobster. A closet cannot eat.

I am always surprised at the number of people who get the lobster all cooked and then have no idea what to do with it. Some hit the lobster with a hammer. All the gray gummy stuff inside comes out. At this point they decide that the lobster is bad and throw it away. Oh how I wish I could tell them what to do. Well, I can't tell them, but I can tell you. I have learned over the years by observation and by listening to my owner.

First you pull off the little legs growing along the side of the body. One of my guests sucks the meat out of these, but most people throw them into the sculch bucket. Sculch is all the lobster garbage. The stuff you don't eat. It is best kept contained in one place or it gets strewn all over, and in a day or two it starts to smell. I remember once someone stored sculch in me—but that is a story I prefer not to remember.

Next, take off the rubber bands, and break off the front claws. You will need a nutcracker or a hammer to crack the claw shell and get out the meat. I have observed that there are two types of lobster eaters. One type collects all the lobster meat on the plate and does not eat anything until all the cracking and picking is done. The other type follows a cycle of crack, pick, and eat; crack, pick, and eat. Most of my visitors are the latter type.

Finally the tail is tackled. This takes real skill, and most of my guests never get it right. Squeeze the sides of the tail between your cupped hands. Hear the pop as the undershell breaks. Then turn the

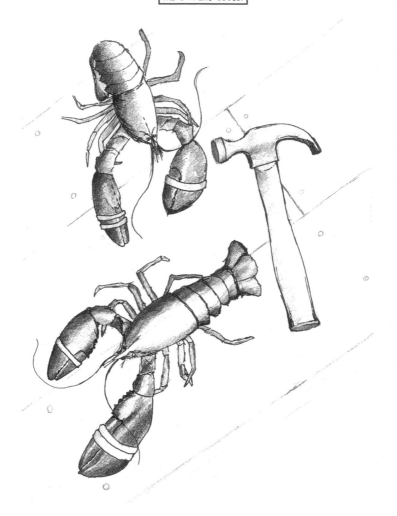

tail inside out. The tail meat pops right out. At least it does for Dr. Jim, but most folks have considerable difficulty with this maneuver. This does not surprise me, as I have often observed that things that Dr. Jim finds easy and even mundane, other folks find complicated and sometimes even scary.

At last the lobster meat is free from the shell. Conversation stills as it is eaten, sometimes alone but usually with lemon or melted butter. I have often wondered why lobster causes short-term muteness. It must be a side effect.

Step Four: Getting Rid of the Lobster

Getting rid of lobster is almost as difficult as getting lobster. You might think that you could just put it in the garbage. Unfortunately, those masked marauders, raccoons, have a passion for lobster. I don't know why. I have never heard of a raccoon setting a lobster trap. Just the same, they love lobster and will tip over garbage cans, tear up boxes, and chew through rope and bungee cords, all to get to the sculch. The result is garbage and sculch everywhere.

Over the years, I have observed one sculch removal system that works well. One of my visitors called it the ecological approach. I call this the gull approach. All the sculch is placed on newspapers or in an open box on the deck. The raccoons usually do not like going up stairs so they stay away.

Sometime during the night or early morning, the sea gulls that hang around the Co-op spy the sculch. I guess the red color helps, or maybe they smell it. Soon flocks of gulls come sweeping down. I really enjoy this, as the gulls do not often come to visit. Quickly they peck the shells clean. There is not a scrap left.

Unfortunately no one ever taught the gulls to be tidy, so shells are scattered over the deck and into the yard. But they are clean shells of no interest to raccoons. They can be gathered, placed in the garbage can, and then taken to the dump.

So now you have it, the annual lobster ritual. As you can see, having lobster is complicated and stressful. People who have never had lobster or have only ordered it in a restaurant badly underrate the whole treatment. It is difficult and can be filled with anticipation, fear, and stress. It is certainly not as simple as it seems.

No One Ever Tells Me Anything

Now that you know a bit about the people I know best, let me tell you about last winter. It was a sad, lonely time from September to November. Winter came too soon; an early storm left six inches of snow on the old lobster trap on the deck. I was cold and lonely—more lonely than usual. I had expected Jan and Kay in early October, but the house stayed empty. The sale at the Ladybug shop came and went, and still they did not come. Even the sale at L.L. Bean was over. I had given up hope by late October. Sometimes that happens. Friends just drift away.

That snowfall was in November. I knew they would never come. No one ever comes during the cold and dreary short days that mark the beginning of winter. One afternoon while slumbering I dreamt that I heard stomping on the steps—no, it was not a dream. There was a click in the lock. It was not my women friends, but my owner. He was here by himself. He turned on Maine Public Radio and made a pot of beans. He opened me, pushed aside paints and canvas, and finally found the bottle of Lochan Ora in my back corner.

I was impatient. I wanted to know what was happening but he was alone and did not talk. Of course, being an owner's closet, I could not ask. I was frustrated.

The days went by. I observed him coming and going, adding some paint to the windowsills, replacing a plank on the deck. It was nice to have company, even silent company, and I did like the music on the radio.

When I was just about to burst of curiosity, Ron and Eve came for dinner. These are old friends from Dr. Jim's university days. They all came to the island as youngsters, and a few years ago Ron and Eve moved back. They now have a lovely house where some famous cook

named Childs use to have her birthdays. They had visited my house frequently over the years, and it was good to see them. Finally I could hear some talk and laughter. Ron talked about real estate prices. Wow,

I never knew that my house was so valuable. I knew I had better be good. Eve talked about some of her stranger clients. She is a rental agent for off-island folks. Would you believe that someone left after only one day because there was not a high-speed Internet connection in the house? Why did they ever go on vacation? Others bitterly complained because in many places cell phones don't work.

Eve also said that her friend Mary was now feeling fine. Last year she had breast cancer and had to drive up to Bangor every day to get shot with some sort of rays. What a drag! They finally got around to talking about what I really wanted to hear about, my friends Jan and Kay.

I didn't believe my shelves. Did they really say that? I would have to listen more carefully.

It seemed that Kay had cancer and had begun some treatment. They kept talking about "chemo." I did not really understand. Cancer scared me. My owner said that she was very tired and did not have any hair. Maybe chemo is a type of hair coloring, like bleach, that went wrong. Some things I know and some things I don't. No one had ever discussed this chemo thing before, at least not that I remembered. All I knew was that I was really worried. Sure wish I could ask questions sometimes.

The crab cakes were eaten. The wine was drunk. The blueberry cobbler was devoured. The candles were burning low, and it was snowing again.

Then it was just my owner and me. He rearranged me a bit before leaving, moving the old button box to one side so as to have enough room for paint and books. The Lochan Ora was put away for the next visit. How I wished I could have asked questions.

Dr. Jim left. I wondered about my friend Kay. I could only wait to learn what happened. Time seemed to slow down that winter. It just crept along. I knew that spring would come. It always does, and with it, new leaves and new guests, and the lobster boats would go out again.

The cycle repeats. I did not know if my friends would return. I hoped so. I hoped that Kay's hair would grow back. I would just have to wait until October and see for myself. No one ever told me anything.

Repairs

By early December all was quiet. I knew that the other houses, the ones that are lived in, were all decorated for the holidays. It was early, but they do a lot of decorating up here—go all out, as they say. The summer folks were long gone. The boats had all been pulled from the water and put in the yards in front of houses. The lily pond was frozen, and all the stores on Main Street were closed, save for one. There was not much left to do except to decorate.

What I really want to tell you is that I was stuffed—really stuffed. You see, when Dr. Jim came up in early November, he fixed me up. He does this every year to repair any damage that has occurred to my house during the summer. He scraped, sanded, trimmed, and scrubbed. He often uses weed killer in the yard, but he couldn't because of that early snow. I really hate that stuff but it is necessary if my house is not to become overgrown with crab grass. Oh yes, he fixed me up just great. I was ready to survive the winter.

But about being stuffed. He also decided to paint. He seems to like this. He paints and sketches boats, trees, buildings, and water— just about anything. This requires canvas, stretcher bars, frames, wires, clips, scissors, hammers, and Exact-o knives, and of course pens, ink, paint, and brushes. He does a good job, my doctor does. He even gets other people to buy some of the things he paints. I also heard him telling friends that he was doing sketches for a book. But then, as he always does, he left for the other coast. Of course all of

77

his stuff got put into me.

I have to guard his things and act happy until he returns, because only he and a few other special people, who won't move these things have the key. If this were not bad enough, last year he did not limit his painting to canvas. He decided to paint my house and me. One day off he went up island, over the bridge up Highway 18. Actually, there are not many other ways to go. Finally he got to Ellsworth, where they have such things, they tell me, as paint stores. When he returned, he arrived with cans and cans of paint.

Until then, I had thought he had good sense, but I swear that he chose the paint by name not color: Quarry Red, Rock of Ages, Deep Water. At least they all have something to do with the Island. It was good of him to remember the quarry. As I told you, for many years the village men quarried granite from the island shores. Some say that you can see it today in the big buildings in Washington, even the capitol building. I have never been there.

My doctor never finished painting, so I was stuffed with paint. As I said, I understood some of this painting, but I sure wished it had been finished. The walls of my house were painted in something called Paper Napkin and my door was Quarry Red. Cans and cans of both colors were sitting on my floor, as well as a dozen partly painted canvases. Of course I knew he would be back to finish. He always does. After all, he made me.

Community

Over the years, my owner and many guests have talked about going to the Wheatleys' home for Tuesday evening cocktails. In fact, the Wheatleys, Ned and Carol, were here long before me. They moved to the island more than 30 years ago when they bought the old boarding house (as I have heard it, that was the polite name) high up on the hill. Over the years they made this old gray house their home, and it has become home for generations of friends. The top floor is an attic that stores more things than I like to think about. The next floor is the Wheatleys' summer home. Here they have a wonderful view of the town, harbor, and all the islands for miles and miles. The next lowest floor, second from the bottom, is sparsely furnished and serves as guest rooms. My owner says that here one can really see how the house was used in the past. The bottom floor is another apartment where the Wheatleys move each October to avoid the cost of heating the whole house. Each apartment is full of books, for Ned and Carol are avid readers.

Ned and Carol, while still considered off-islanders, have become part of the fabric of island life. Ned helped to put in the first streetlights. Carol became the mainstay of several island groups, including the quilting society. In her later years, after taking a fall on an icy winter morning, Carol was not able to get around well, but she still was able to use email to provide her many friends around the world with her daily island weather forecast. In Finland, Delaware, California, and a host of other places, people would awaken daily to learn about the foibles of island weather: Nor'easters, hail storms, the first day it gets above freezing, and the wolf moon of fall. Carol wrote about all of these. Then one day, there was a new message, this time from Ned. Carol had died in her sleep shortly after sending her last weather forecast.

It had always been a regular Tuesday night tradition among the Wheatleys' friends (and friends of friends) to have cocktails with Ned and Carol. In the summer this could be a party of more than a dozen that dwindled to five or six during the cold days of winter. Before you start picturing a grand party, I had better explain that cocktails are actually boxed wine and scotch, but that is not important. What is important is the Tuesday night gathering.

With Carol gone, it is just Ned and he, or so they say, is ever more forgetful. Everyone worries about him but he is firmly independent. Now on Tuesday evenings, everyone brings a little something to eat. There is always too much so at the end of the evening Ned's refrigerator is full of food. During the week, a relative or neighbor often drops in with food or calls to ask if Ned needs anything.

Sometimes it takes a community to remain independent.

Nevertheless, on Tuesday evenings Ned and Scotch reign supreme. The talk is of island gossip. What are the prices of houses? Is the new restaurant any good? Is the island ever going to get its own policeman? How is Old Man Radlaw doing? Off-island visitors are always welcome. They add spice and variety from the outside world, telling of their adventures and asking what would seem like silly questions. Tuesday night at Ned's is always the same and ever-changing. As I hear about all of this, I learn a little more about the importance of community.

Hibernation

Very few of my guests visit during hibernation time. This is official-ly from just after Christmas to late April, but actually begins ear-lier and may last later. In fact, hibernation usually begins about the time the Ladybug store closes. But I am getting ahead of myself.

You might wonder about how I know about hibernation. I lis-ten. My guests often talk about this, especially those who come during the cold. Besides, with the Lobster Co-op just down the hill, I can hear the daily conversation of the lobstermen as they come and go.

I always know when hibernation is about to start. The days may be sunny and warm, but the lobstermen begin to pull their traps, and I can see them pass my house with trucks stacked high with traps. Starting in early October, more and more traps leave the water and take up residence outside the houses of the lobstermen. At first I thought that the lobster left the water too, but I have learned that this is not the case. All over the island there are piles of traps and piles of colorful buoys. There is a different color combination for each lob-sterman. Also there are lots and lots of coils of multicolored ropes. At the same time, the number of off-island visitors dwindles until the locals can walk down the middle of Main Street, all two blocks, only occasionally dodging a car or truck. Not much is open. One by one the shops slowly close down. First the Ladybug shop closes, then the others. The bookmark lady packs her car and heads north to her win-ter home. (Yes, some folks do head north for the winter.) The *New York Times* is no longer available on Sunday; the restaurants adver-tise their fall closing schedules in the newspaper. By November, most everything is closed except the post office, a shop or two, and of course the grocery store.

Now you would think that with all this inactivity things would be very dull, but this is not the case at all. This is the time of year when all community activities get going.

First there are the church suppers: haddock, boiled beef, and baked beans. These are the staples. What people really go for are the desserts. Here our local ladies and a few gents really shine. You name it, and if it is good and sweet, they make it. Apple and blueberry pies are favorites, but Mrs. Redman makes a wonderful coconut cake. Another center of island social life is the Friday night movies. Like many small towns, mine has an ancient opera house left over from the quarry boom days. For many years it sat on a hill cold and unused. Then two ladies from off-island saw possibilities that no one else had seen before. They came, cleaned, painted, cleaned, insulated, and cleaned until the place shone—or at least was usable. I have heard my guests say that many mice were made homeless.

During the summer the opera house has shows almost every night: movies, plays, music groups, and jugglers—you name it. These are mainly for the off-islanders who are here visiting and need something to do with their children in the evenings.

In the hibernation, things change. There is a different movie every weekend. These are not first-run movies. They are a means to community. People can get the latest movies on DVD, but it's only at the opera house that they can see their friends, munch on real popcorn, and see *The Bride of Frankenstein* right before Halloween or *White Christmas* in mid-December. The opera house has become a center of community social life.

There is more to hibernation than social life. Once the lobsters are left to their winter sleep, many folks turn to wreath making. You know those Christmas catalogues you get advertising fresh Maine balsam wreaths? Have you ever thought where they come from? Well duh, Maine. But have you ever seen a wreath factory? Well neither have I, nor have any of the people who ever visited here.

Many of the wreaths, thousands in fact, come from my island. The trees provide the balsam branches that are harvested each year with care to not kill the trees. In homes all over the island, the branches are cut and shaped into wreaths over metal rings. Then large red or blue bows are attached along with pinecones and other extras. Each day from mid-November to almost Christmas, trucks from the various shipping services carry away a small part of my forests. Somehow my balsam arrives at your (or your friends') home to welcome in the holiday season. At the same time the income from selling the wreaths helps heat the homes of my island. The income also provides Christmas dinner and, oh yes, not a few Christmas gifts. It has always made me feel good to know that even in winter, my island can be shared with my summer visitors.

After the holidays pass, the hibernation becomes even deeper. Very few lobstermen leave the warmth of their homes. The few shops that stayed opened until Christmas are now closed. Life centers on school athletes and an excellent school chess club. Our seventeen local churches do their bit to keep the social scene active, and snowmobiles become the favorite means of transportation. Many of my residents take vacations and visit owner's closets in the south. All in all the pace slows, and everyone is looking at the catalogues and ordering their spring flowers.

In many ways hibernation is a time of renewal. It is the time that island folks remember who they are, make friends again with each other, and prepare to welcome off-island guests. Life is a little like that, looking inward, looking outward in a regular cycle.

Waiting

Waiting is one of the things I do best. You see, most of the time I am alone. There are no visitors in my house from November to June, except maybe at Christmas, when there are sometimes a few days of excitement and lots of colored paper. My owner comes only a few weeks a year. Even when there are people visiting my house, they are mostly gone. So I wait, always interested in what will happen next, even a little anxious. Will old friends or my owner return? Will there be first-time visitors, and if so, will they like the house or find fault?

The most anxious times are waiting for a storm. I can always feel it coming in my boards but never know exactly what it will be like. Sometimes it is gentle rain or a lovely soft snow. Other times it is howling wind, driving rain, and waves crashing across the harbor and onto the pier at the Lobster Co-op. I always worry about these storms. Will they blow out a window or, worse yet, blow the roof off my house? If the water and wind get inside, they can really cause damage. If they cause too much damage, then my owner might tear me down. When I think like this I can get really terrified. It is funny how little things can set one off.

But then I remember that I have seen many storms, and they have passed with great excitement but little damage. Why just last year a big one blew through, and I heard a dreaded crash. I had heard the lobstermen shouting that a boat had gone down. This made me worry more. For a long time I did not know what had happened, and I just waited and worried.

It began to feel damp and very cold. I worried more. I thought that mold was growing in my corners. No one told me anything. I imagined all kinds of terrible things. Thankfully, after a few weeks of waiting, I heard footsteps on my deck, the key in the lock, and joy, my owner, the doctor, arrived.

He immediately felt the cold and damp and went to investigate. This is something that closets cannot do. He quickly returned, as my entire house is quite small. I heard him calling someone on the telephone. From what I could gather, the dormer window in my house's upstairs bedroom had been blown out in the storm. The bed was wet, and the floorboards had buckled.

My owner got right to work fixing things. He heated me up real good to get rid of the damp. Soon he was washing all the sheets and rugs. He opened me to take out some bleach, which he used to kill the mold. Guess this mold can be really nasty if you don't control it. Soon the friendly repairman who helped build me came and put in a new window. I could hear him whistling and hammering. The house said that it didn't hurt a bit.

All at once I realized that everything was OK. All that worrying had been for nothing. It hadn't helped at all. This time everything was OK. Just the same, when I have to wait, I worry.

Another Year

The summer has come and gone. I had several interesting guests. Even the Grays returned, to my surprise. They seemed much happier and did not complain about flagmen. I guess they are getting the hang of the place.

Now it is after midnight in mid-October with waning moon and stars. My last guest left ten days ago. All is quiet. Many of the lobster boats have been taken from the water. I was so hoping my friends Jan and Kay would come. It has been more than two years since I have seen them. It is getting colder, and there has been lots of rain. I guess I will just have to settle in for the winter.

I must admit to being sad and lonely. I really miss my friends. For years they came every year like clockwork. They always arrived just in time for the sale at the Ladybug store. But then last year they did not come. When Dr. Jim came in May this year, I head him talking to someone on the phone, and he again mentioned something about Kay having cancer. Now Kay and Jan are not here again. I am really worried and very, very sad. It is hard to lose friends. I know that closets should not feel this way. After all, people come and go all the time. Just the same, when they came back year after year and loved me the way they did, I couldn't help myself. I would cry if I could.

Oh my goodness! What is this I hear? Is it really a key in the door? YES! I hear tired voices. Seems they took a wrong turn and almost drove to Ellsworth. Finally they saw the red horse and knew they were almost there. Could it be? It is! It is! My friends have returned. I am so happy and so embarrassed. No one cleaned me after my last visitors. (This is something I just can't do myself.) The beds are rumpled and unmade; the used towels were tossed carelessly in the washing machine; sour milk sits in the refrigerator. Oh my, this is not the way it is supposed to be. Sometimes I wish I wasn't a closet. I want to welcome them. I want to hug them.

However, Kay and Jan do not seem disturbed. In fact, they do not seem to mind a bit. I think that they are as happy to be here as I am to see them. They examine every corner of the house and even peek inside me. Thankfully, they turn on the heat. Kay's hair is short, but I can see that there is definitely hair. Before I can even calm down from the unexpected excitement of seeing them again, they have snuggled in their beds and gone off to sleep. As for me, I am much too excited to sleep. I am so happy they have returned, and I have so much I wish I could tell them.

Several days have passed. Kay and Jan have been up to their usual ritual. Each day they get up early, do a little reading or writing, and have a wonderful breakfast before starting out on an exploration. My house almost always smells good with their cooking. Today it is raining, so they have built a fire in the cast iron stove. Each has been attending to work, mostly reading and writing. I so like the homey peace. There is nothing like the companionship of gentle quiet. At last Kay stretches and tells Jan she wants to read to her what she has been writing. Since she is sitting just outside my door, I can hear too. She reads

> I am the owner's closet. You might know me. I am at the very core of a vacation house on an island off the coast of Maine. My owner, a doctor who lives far away, puts all his belongings in me. At least he puts in the belongings that he does not want others to use. I keep them safe from the parade of visitors. I will tell you more about these folks later, but first I want to tell you a little about myself and how I came into being.

Yes, she is writing about me. I am so happy.

88

WHAT A DIFFERENCE

Now I am the person I have become,
The person left behind is gone, yet here.
About a year; what a difference it makes.
The exhaustion's gone, but not forgotten,
Replaced by fear, repressed but barely so.
Now I am the person I have become.
The cycle continues, as it surely must-
The laughter and sorrow sharply focused.
About a year; what a difference it makes.
I sleep nights, and daily wake with wonder.

Slowly I walk, pain my companion.
Now I am the person I have become.
The changes are not those that others see;
To them I am the same, if only more so.
About a year; what a difference it makes.
If we notice every year is the same,
The lifetime left behind is gone, yet here.
Now I am the person I have become.
About a year; what a difference it makes.

—KRL